News Today!

by Kim Riley
illustrated by Wednesday Kirwan

Harcourt
SCHOOL PUBLISHERS

Printed in China

ISBN 10: 0-15-350454-4
ISBN 13: 978-0-15-350454-9

Ordering Options
ISBN 10: 0-15-350333-5 (Grade 3 Below-Level Collection)
ISBN 13: 978-0-15-350333-7 (Grade 3 Below-Level Collection)
ISBN 10: 0-15-357466-6 (package of 5)
ISBN 13: 978-0-15-357466-5 (package of 5)

2 3 4 5 6 7 8 9 10 985 15 14 13 12 11 10 09 08 07

Characters

Lara   **Taylor**   **Megan**

Eric   **Kevin**

Mr. Francis, school principal

Ms. Flanagan, school librarian

Setting: A school television studio

Lara: Good morning, I'm Lara Roberts. This is the Greenville School Network.

Taylor: I'm Taylor Smith. The big story today is this afternoon's pep rally. Let's go to our sports reporter, Megan Moore.

3

Megan: Hi, Taylor. I'm at the gym. The assembly will be held here this afternoon. We will meet the members of the basketball team. We'll see their new uniforms for the first time. Then the team will play a short game for the viewers.

4

Lara: How does the team look this year, Megan?

Megan: I think we can expect a very successful season. You can't dismiss our chances to make it to the championship.

Taylor: Thank you, Megan. Now let's go to our special guest, our principal, Mr. Francis.

Mr. Francis: I have a very special announcement. Next month we'll hold a World's Fair.

Lara: A World's Fair? Will people from around the world come to our school?

Mr. Francis: Well, no.

Taylor: Will we have events for every country in the world?

Mr. Francis: Not quite. We will try to have as many as possible, though.

Lara: Who is putting this all together?

Mr. Francis: Our students are our resources. Each class will prepare a display that will tell about a different culture. You'll research the topics in your social studies classes.

Taylor: Is this really just homework that looks like a fair?

Mr. Francis: It's a fun learning experience. Local businesses have donated prizes for students to win. A musical guest will perform.

Lara: Is it someone famous?

Mr. Francis: Yes. You'll want to get her autograph!

Taylor: We'll keep reporting on this in days to come. World's Fair—fun or homework?

Mr. Francis: It's fun!

Lara: Thanks, Mr. Francis. Now let's go to Kevin Burke with the weather.

Kevin: It's another pleasant day with blue skies and sunshine!

Taylor: What about this weekend?

Kevin: It looks like heavy rain again.

Lara: Why does it always rain on weekends?

Kevin: It doesn't, Lara. It's just a coincidence when it rains on weekends.

Lara: I call it bad luck. Thanks, Kevin— I guess.

Taylor: Lara, we have breaking news! Let's go to Eric Flores in the library.

Eric: This is very exciting. Iggy the Iguana, the third-grade class pet, has been found! She's safe and in good shape.

Lara: What happened, Eric?

Eric: Iggy disappeared yesterday during class chores, while her cage was being cleaned. A school-wide search failed to find her—until today! Let's talk to Ms. Flanagan, the school librarian. Ms. Flanagan, where did you find Iggy?

Ms. Flanagan: I was watering the library plants. Suddenly, I saw a leaf move! Iggy was concealed in the leaves. The green leaves acted as a camouflage. It made her almost invisible.

Eric: How did she survive?

Ms. Flanagan: She was able to get both food and water from the plants.

Eric: That's a very independent iguana! Thanks, Ms. Flanagan.

Ms. Flanagan: Remember, the library has many books about iguanas!

Taylor: Well, this has been a very exciting news morning, Lara!

Lara: It certainly has. Thanks for watching the Greenville School Network, the only place for school news!

Think Critically

1. What is the setting of this Readers' Theater?

2. How do you know who is speaking?

3. What do the students have to do for the World's Fair?

4. How does Lara feel about Kevin's weather report?

5. Who would you like to be on a newscast—a news reporter, a sports reporter, or a weather reporter? Why?

 Science

Iguana Info In this play, a lost iguana is found. Look up some information about iguanas. Write some facts on note cards. Share what you find with classmates.

School-Home Connection Choose a few pages from this book. Divide parts between yourself and a family member. Then read the newscast together for other members of the family.

Word Count: 541